Between a death and a hard place

A collection of short stories, flash fiction and
poems for the darker nature

Published by Insomnia Knights Productions,
Nottingham, England

Although the stories in this collection are fiction, and about no one in particular they do touch on themes of a darker nature. Themes within this book may cause unwanted reactions and trigger emotional responses for some readers. The author in no way wants to upset or cause offence.

It's never too late to talk, to open up about problems we face and if anything in this work hits a little too close to home, then please, tell someone, anyone. The darkness is out there, even inside of us, but that does not mean there is no light, and we should all try our best to defeat the darkness. And there are people out there trying to help.

If any of the themes hit too close to home talk to somebody:

www.samaritans.org

www.papyrus-uk.org

www.romper.com

www.cruse.org.uk

www.standingtogether.org.uk

www.shelter.org.uk

this is not an exclusive list and there are many more charities worldwide that are here to help.

Contents

Introduction

Before this anthology came together it started out as an idea, a series of short stories and extracts that would give me a chance to look at what stories I wanted to tell. I had created a few ideas that became the start of full-length novels, or even excerpts that I thought I would find a home for at a later date, but then with a few turns in fate this collection grew. From my first piece of flash fiction "The longest day" an ember was lit beneath me and the stories that appear in this work began to blossom.

Now I know that the works in this book are not of the happy, friendly variety. But this work became an outlet for those little tales that had no real home anywhere else. From my second piece "Brotherly love" that appeared in a college anthology entitled "In the shadow of the castle", I knew that this was a collection that I wanted to create. So here it is, my first collection of short works, from college anthologies to prize entries. I give to you:

"Between a death and a hard place"

Prose

Longest day

This piece of flash fiction was written whilst I was sat on a bus to work one day, the final draft was almost an exact copy of the hand scribbled story I wrote on that bumpy bus ride. Although it has never been published before, it was however, the first piece that I shared which is why I decided to place it as the first story in the anthology.

Brotherly love

My college entry into "In the shadow of the castle" this work was written over a very short deadline, from concept to completion. I knew what I wanted the story to be, Love, Betrayal, and a sibling rivalry this story has a classic feel without the classic telling.

Devoid

An allegory on depression, this work was written more for my own understanding than for anyone else. A story of the loneliness that we can all sometimes feel "Devoid" is my attempt to visualise what it is to be truly lost. Written in an airport departure lounge it was easy to feel what it was like to be surrounded by people and yet feel alone.

The dream

This one is almost autobiographical, well as autobiographical as me telling you about a dream that I had can be. The vivid detail that I can remember the dream even years later is the reason I put pen to paper on this one. Originally, I was planning on using this one in another project, a novel called Déjà vu, however as that project dwindled into the ether, I decided to share this part with the world.

Falling walls

A semi-autobiographical metaphor, this is a look at how we hide behind walls and how we strengthen these walls each time we have to build them back up. Written as a quickfire piece of flash fiction I wrote it under the guise that I may extend it one day in the future.

The long road

An allegory of the decisions we make, this tale of a man going on an adventure allowed me to look inwards, allowed me to look at the way I made choices in my life and how they led me to where I am today.

The affair

Something as simple as turning over your phone when they walk in, switching off the display, even a cagey muttering can leave a dark thought in someone's mind, the affair looks at this, at the way we build up evidence in our minds when something doesn't add up.

Fear of the dark

Whenever things in life troubled me, I always found it impossible to sleep, voices would shout at me, trick my brain into thinking the worse case scenario about everything. This was written on one such night when I was trying to silence the voices by keeping myself busy. As I watched the hours tick by and the next day begin to loom, I felt a sense of dread that this would happen the next night and the one after that.

Trouble in Auldrun

This started as a story I told myself whilst walking home one evening. It is loosely set in the town I lived in and was meant to be the start of a larger story. A brief snippet of a much larger story that may one day be extended. This practice has been a constant over my writing carrier as a way to see if a story was able to be developed further.

The game

Riding along a dark road on my way to work at 3AM each morning; I started to think how no one would know if anything happened to me for a few hours, when the morning traffic would begin to flow. One thought led to another and the story of the game was born. This short story took on a life of its own however and quickly became my first full length novel. Joust.

The darkness

This one took a couple of years to finish, a lot happened in my life between the first time I tried to put these feelings into words and the moment I felt strong enough to share them. It is a look at the way I, like many others, overthink a situation and allow myself to be drawn in to the worst narrative possible. It is a key feature and feeling of what drove me to write this collection in the first place.

Poetry

I would never call myself a poet, in fact poetry was always furthest from my mind when it came to writing and to being an author however I was challenged to write a poem for entry into my college anthology and I kept that challenge going for myself long after the course was done.

A letter to my unborn child

As the title suggests this work came out of a low point in my life. My first child, something that I had never really considered before, was unfortunately never meant to be and my fiancée and I lost the baby before it ever had chance to be much more than an idea. But that idea was one that I fell in love with, it did not take the child's birth for me to fall in love, and this poem was my way of understanding the feelings that I was having.

Silver linings

A quick exercise to get an idea down on paper ended in this poem, it was never intended as much more than a concept, eventually become a full story however after completing it I decided that I would share it as I believe that it carries an important message about how we look at ourselves and our past when wc are going through hard times.

In the shadow of the castle

The title was a college anthology that I was a part of, and this poem was going to be my second submission. However, I never sent it in and over the years forgot about it. a short poem about the homeless of my home city; I had intended on making it much longer.

Prose

Longest day

I carefully slide the key into the front door and wince as I hear the lock slam open, its late and the last thing that I want is to wake you. Without turning on the lights I find myself in unfamiliar surroundings. The furniture looks different in this light and the photos of our happy family are almost unrecognisable. I think to myself how tired I am, and this must be why everything feels a little off. I continue into the dining room and place my things on our new table, the curtains are open and the moonlight shines brightly in here and everything starts to feel a little normal, a little more like home. I strip off my clothes and put them in the machine ready for the morning and take a cold beer from the fridge, cursing under my breath because this isn't the brand that I like, I open it anyway and take a small sip.

Now I head upstairs; pushing my feet tight against the wall to stop the creaking and once at the top I slip inside our bedroom. This has always been the darkest room of the house and so I cannot see where I am walking, I stub my toe on the corner of the bed, stifling my shrieks of pain I hobble over to the bedside and find you laying across the bed, I reach out and gently brush my fingers across your arm causing you to stir. I take this chance to kiss you on your cheek and hold you tightly so that you know that I will never let you go and with another swift kiss on the cheek I get up, grab a used towel off of the radiator and head down the hall to the bathroom flipping the shower on as I go.

I finish stripping down and put my last few items of clothing in a pile on the floor, knowing how much you hate this I remind myself to move them afterwards and step into the shower. As I rub myself down, I realise that all of my shower gel has gone so I pick up one of your more floral scented bottles and begin to clean myself. The hot water washes away the pain and stress of the long day and I find myself enjoying this a little too much.

Once I am clean and relaxed, I step out of the shower, wrap a towel around my waist and walk back out onto the landing. I decide to look in on our daughter and find myself ducking into her room. Once I am beside her bed, I give her the same reassuringly tight squeeze that I gave her mother then take her in my arms and carry her to your bedside. Gently placing her in your arms I round the bed stopping at your dresser to take out the painkillers that you keep there and taking what I need to dull the pain I finish my beer in one go, dropping my towel I slide between the cold sheets and with one last kiss, this time on your soft lips, I tell you that I love you and lay back to join you in the land of eternal slumber.

Brotherly love

It had been a month since Matthew had been home, a month away for work, but now he was back. He was a day early and although he had planned to call Amanda and tell her that he was almost there he decided that he would surprise her. He had gotten off the train and decided to take the bus so that she would not know that he was home. Thoughts of their reunion had filled his mind the whole way back, thinking about how he would take her to dinner to her favourite place, a little Japanese restaurant that they had gone to on their first date. After getting off the bus a few stops early so that he could pick up her favourite flowers, Lilly's, to make sure that he did not arrive empty handed, he finally approached the corner of the street. He could feel himself smiling, he was genuinely excited to be home. Work had been terrible, he was sure he was about to get fired but right now, that did not matter. All that mattered to him was that he was home. He walked between two parked vans and out into the middle of the road, just as his front door opened. Like a deer caught in headlights, he froze for a second sure that he was about to be spotted and ruin the surprise, jumping backwards between the two vehicles so as not to be spotted he disappeared just in time to see Amanda walking out of the house.

"I'll see you later then?" he heard her asking someone back in the house and Matthew tried to lean out to see who it was, but he couldn't quite see without walking back into the road.

"You can see me now," came the reply, and as he was about to walk out and expose himself, he saw his brother exit the apartment and walk out towards Amanda. His brother was shirtless, and his skin glistened with sweat as he walked over to Amanda, took her in one of his arms and planted a huge kiss on her lips. Matthew could see that this was not the first time the two of them had kissed, that they were all too familiar with one another and he fell backwards. Placing his head between his knees and taking deep and yet rapid breaths he tried to explain what he had just witnessed in a way that didn't make him feel sick.

At least an hour had passed before Matthew was able to control himself, he had thought up every scenario that he possibly could by the time he stood up. He knew that there would be some good explanation that he had not thought of. There was absolutely no way that Amanda was having an affair with his brother. He stood up, brushed himself off and headed towards his home. As he reached the door, he took another deep and calming breath and walked inside. The house seemed so strange to him Amanda had always been house proud, everything had its place and there was never any mess anywhere, however now there was food still on the table. Two places set. There were multiple piles of clothes left lying around on the floor, beer cans and wine bottles lined the side of the sink. The state of the place had distracted him so much that he didn't realise that the shower had been running, or that it had stopped.

"Matthew?" the sound of surprise in his brothers' voice stunned him and made him jump in equal measure. "I thought you was getting back tomorrow," he continued.

"Clearly," Matthew replied, his eyes darting around the house to the mess that was spread all over.

"Yeah, sorry about all the mess," his brother proclaimed innocently. "Amanda let me crash here for a few days whilst you were out of town," his voice trailed as he tried to find the right words. "My place is erm," he started but was quickly cut off.

"Too far from Amanda I suppose," he hadn't meant to say it, and most certainly not with as much venom as he did but Matthew knew that the words needed to be said.

"What…" his brother started but he knew there was no point.

"I saw you Simon, I saw both of you outside just now," his temper was growing, and he could feel himself shaking as he tried to hold back. "How long?" he shouted, unable to stop himself any longer. "How long have the two of you been at it? How long have you been betraying me?" his anger forced a tear to escape and run down his cheek.

"I'm sorry little brother, I didn't mean..." his weak attempt to diffuse the situation just made Matthew even angrier.

"You didn't mean to? You didn't mean to what? What exactly didn't you mean to do? Tell me!"

The series of questions was too quick to allow Simon to answer, but that was fine by him. He had no answer. Nothing he could say could make this right.

"So, you have nothing to say?" Matthew began again.

"No," was all the sound Simon could muster, however seeing that this was not enough of an answer he started again to try to break the silence. "She...she..." the words were there but he still struggled to say them.

"What? She what?" Matthew demanded, his hands beginning to ball into fists as he spoke.

"She hasn't been happy for years," the words almost felt like a relief for Simon to say and he was soon able to continue. "You don't appreciate her when you're here, you are gone for work more and more. You make her feel terrible for wanting a life, but then you don't want to go anywhere or do anything with her."

His words flowed easier with every breath and it was soon apparent to them both that he wasn't finished but Matthew knew that he needed to interject, he had to stop his brother from saying these things. From saying these lies.

"ENOUGH!" he shouted, to which an instant silence fell across the room. "no matter what I have done, it did not give you the right to do this to me. You were my brother, MY brother. You should not have done it; you had no right." A single tear formed in his eye again and he stormed off into the bathroom so that his brother would not see him cry.

When he returned from the bathroom his brother was gone and he looked around at all the mess that was left. Frantically he began to clean, clearing all the rubbish away first and then putting everything back in its place. He washed the floors, the walls and even scrubbed the lamp clean. As he returned everything back the way it was meant to be. He had barely finished when he heard keys jingling in the front door, and as Amanda realised that it wasn't locked, she let herself in. entering the house Amanda was shocked to find Matthew standing there.

"He's gone," Matthew said as she entered the room, his voice filled with sorrow. "He has left us both and is not coming back."

His words shocked Amanda as she had always thought hers' and Simon's affair had been a secret.

"What do you mean?" she asked wearily, and with a tone of forced confusion "where has he gone? Why would he leave you?" her questions rolled off her tongue with ease, but she could feel the strain of trying to sound confused and innocent as she said them.

"I mean he has gone; he has left for good, and he will never be returning." The sharp tone in his voice took Amanda back and she stood in silence as she waited for him to speak again.

"And he left me for the same reason that he left you," his words were filled with hatred now and Amanda knew that her secret was a secret no more. She stepped forward her hand outstretched hoping to calm him with her touch but as she neared, he spun around suddenly, and she jumped back in shock.

The hatred in his eyes however, seemed to disappear as soon as he looked upon her face and was replaced by his usual soft look.

"I am not mad at you, at either of you, I understand that I have played my part, not given you what you needed. I understand now that he gave you what I couldn't, but things will be different now." He stepped forward as he spoke and gently placed his hand on her cheek, and with a loving look in his eyes he pulled her close and with a forceful passion that had once seemed so alien to him he planted his lips against hers. His arms slipped around her waist as he continued to kiss her, and to his shock her lips began to move in unison with his own. The two lovers embraced as though it was for the first time and they were quickly undressing one another as they moved through the house towards the bedroom. In their lust filled movements they crashed through the furniture knocking things from the shelves as they thudded against the thin walls.

Matthew took her in his arms and carried her the last few feet to the bed, he placed her down and broke away from their kiss so that he could tear the last few items of clothing from her and then from himself and he joined her on the bed. They began to kiss, and Matthew pushed her hands above her head and held them down with one of his own. He felt her back arching as he pushed himself deep inside her and as the two made love with the passion of two young lovers enjoying themselves for the first time, he slid his free hand down, off the side of the bed and grabbed a hold of his brothers' cold dead hand.

Devoid

All I see is black, not the sort of black that one might imagine, like the blackness of a lightless winter's night. No. The blackness that I see is that of the constant emptiness of nothing. I look down to my hands, but cannot see them, they are there, I feel them, but I cannot see them. I stretch out my hand hoping to find something that I can grab a hold of, but I find just empty space before me. I take my first step, trying to discover some way out of the darkness, but I feel no ground beneath my feet. My feet are there, I can feel them as well as I felt my hands, but nothing that they make contact with. No earth beneath my feet.

Another attempt to move appears unfruitful. Twisting and turning I thrash about like I am in a pool but there is no water, only my empty void of absolute nothingness. Determined I try over and over, but I cannot help myself, I feel no movement and the hopelessness starts to set in. Movement has failed me but before I can accept defeat I scream out, hoping that someone else is here in the darkness with me, someone that can help me, explain to me where I am, what this place is. I scream as loud as I can, I feel the air rushing from my body but alas. No sound. "What is this place?" I ask myself, the voice in my mind is so clear that

I believe I hear it. "Help me," I scream again, but still no sound falls upon my ears.

"What is this place?" I ask myself again, knowing now that the voice inside me is the only one that I have. I must not give up, I must continue to thrash about, make noise and hope that I can find a way out. I do not know if it is a minute or an hour, a day or a month, there is no time in this void of mine.

Defeated, I fall back, or at least I think that I do, I have no sense of my movements anymore. Accepting my fate, that I will live in this void forever. Then like an arrow to my heart I have the daunting realization.

"I am dead."

The words form in my mind; however, it is my ears that hear them. The tears begin to well behind my eyes but with them comes a small glimmer of light. My realization has allowed me to see more clearly. With my newfound senses I start to feel the floor beneath my feet, the wind on my face and as I reach out my hand, I feel something. Still, I am unsure of what, but at least now I am not alone, well not as hopelessly alone as I had been before. I take this chance to call out, and in the distance, I hear someone call back, an echo? Another lost soul? It doesn't matter, I am not alone. The knowledge that I am dead has given me the chance to exist again, to live. The contradiction is lost on me, that this is how I feel again, instead I find myself happy that I exist at all.

As my sight becomes clearer, I notice the shadows of people that I know scurrying about in front of me, busy living their lives. They do not see me. Why would they? I am dead after all. I try to interact, but they do not see me, hear me, or even feel my presence.

"This prison is worse," I call to myself, before I did not exist, this world did not exist. Now. I do not exist but the world around me does, there but out of reach. I close my eyes and find myself hoping to feel the void again, but nothing changes, the emptiness is inside me now. I need it not to be, I need it to be out of me, all around me. Now I have a new problem, how do I get the void out? I ask for help, but I receive none, I grab ahold of passersby hoping they can show me the way, but no matter what I try they ignore me. Panicked, I want my void back, better to feel nothing at all than this emptiness, and then I see it, a small key lying on a table. A way out. I pick up the key and to my surprise the keyhole appears on my arm, I know this is how I release the void. I slot the key into its receptacle, twist open the lock and with it the sweet release of the void washes over me. "I am back where I belong" I tell myself as I slide into nothingness this time free of the loneliness, free of my feelings.

"I am dead."

The dream

I was walking down a dark and narrow path, it was so void of light that I could barely see my feet beneath me, only the faint glow of the moonlight occasionally appearing through the gaps in the leafless branches overhead. There was a chill in the air that night, the kind of cold that felt like small needles pressing against your cheeks, and I had my coat wrapped around my face as I walked ever on.

A short way down the path, at least I think it was a short way as I could no longer see where I had come from, I noticed the dim glow of a distant light flickering and it gave me some hope that this path would come to an end soon. With each passing step I drew closer to the light and as the overwhelming embrace of the darkness began to fade away, and so it seemed, did the biting chill in the air.

At last, I reached the source of the light, and discovered that it was the flickering of a bulb atop a large iron bridge. Even though the bridge looked battered and worn, with its cracked lime green paint and faded graffiti, it felt as though I had finally reached somewhere. My mood improved at this sign of civilisation and at the prospect that I would soon be free of this prison of darkness that I had found myself in. however, as I reached the bottom of the stairs, I realised that I was no longer alone. Stood a few short steps ahead was another man, wrapped as I was in a large coat and walking a few steps ahead of me. In my excitement I tried to call out, but no words escaped my trembling mouth. With the failing of my voice, I spurred on, hoping to catch the man before me. Step after step I heard my feet slam against the thick wooden stairs and was surprised that my elusive companion made no move to investigate the echoing bangs behind him or the deathly creaking of the large metal bolts as the wood twisted against them.

Every step felt a little more rushed, my haste making me clumsy as I started to slip on the edge of each of the frost coated wooden stairs, and yet my progress was slow, as though the bridge grew in height as I escalated. I looked back from where I had come, but the unrelenting darkness had swallowed the world behind me. My hope was fading as though this bridge had been placed here to torment me, like tantalus, I found that with each attempt to reach my goal it simple moved another step further away. The bitter cold began to take it hold of me once more and the darkness started to envelop me. Still, I pressed on, determined as ever to reach my goal, to catch the mysterious man that strolled ever on before me. Pulling my coat up around my face again a took both ends of my collar one hand just low enough for me to see where I was trying to go.

At last, my steps began to accelerate, and I drew closer and closer to the man that had thus eluded me, however, as I drew nearer my heart began to feel heavy, my breathing laboured, and my thoughts became clouded in fear. I did not understand why I was feeling this way but still, I marched on. Step after step my fear grew as my proximity to the flickering light diminished and as I reached the last few steps, I had finally caught my mysterious stranger. His coat was similar to mine long and black but a little more worn with age. His collar was turned up as mine was and his hair was long, thick and a silvery white as though he had gone grey many years before and I thought to myself that maybe this was why he hadn't turned around at all the noise that I was making. I reached out my hand to gently touch his shoulder and finally get his attention hoping that the companionship that he would afford me would bring me comfort on this dark night, however, as I reached out my hand, my fingers so close that I could feel the static electricity jumping between us, my body froze, and my heart filled with dread.

He started to turn towards me, with a slowness that boarded on stillness. His gaunt face looking unnaturally old. It was all I could do not to stare. As his eyes met mine on that bitterly cold night, I felt an uneasiness that I had never experienced before and with a single quick move he raised a small gun from out of nowhere. I dropped back in fear; a sense of acceptance washed over me as I prepared for what was about to happen. The last moments of my life would be spent here, on this dark bridge, with its flickering lights and cracked paint. His gaunt features morphed into a wicked smile as he raised the gun and I could see that he had been waiting for this very moment and as I took one last deep breath, he raised the gun to his own temple and.

BANG!

The violent way that I awoke shocked me, my heart was racing, and my breath seemed to be just out of reach. A few small tears had formed in my sleep and where now sat firmly on my cheeks. I looked around the room hoping to figure out where I was and as my eyes adjusted to the light, I realised that I was home, safe and in my bed. The relief that it had all been a dream allowed me to lay back down but the fear that I felt was so real that I could not get back to sleep. My body was as cold as it had been in the dream as I lay there covered in a film of cold sweat from head to toe, I pulled my duvet around me and closed my eyes just hoping I could get back to sleep but I was awake now and nothing was going to change that.

Falling walls

I built my house out of mortar and stone, I measured each wall, lined each beam, and checked them over and over, making sure that they were secure. I knew that it had to be strong if I was ever to let my family inside. Son's, daughter's, wife, all of it, living the good life behind my high walls. We were safe, as long as the walls were strong, we were safe.

I built my house of mortar and stone, nothing was going to penetrate these walls, my family and I were safe. Or so I allowed myself to believe. They say that it is our enemies that teach us to build high walls, however the ones that can do the most damage are your friends. The ones we feel safe enough to let inside our walls, to live with us in our stone palace of security. I had not learned this lesson yet, even though I had received many lessons to prove it.

Like a little pig, my first house was built with straw, I felt safe hiding behind these walls too. Yet, as I was attacked for the very first time my enemies made very short work of its construction and I paid a heavy price. The first time the walls come down they pull your self-belief along with them. This was the first lesson, for although it was my enemies that tore down the walls it was my own flesh and blood that gave them the tools to do it. they did it so that they could draw me back inside their walls, back inside where I was meant to feel safe, however my self-belief had been shattered, weak and alone I clung on to the toxicity that their meagre shelter provided. I hid away, believing that I had failed.

After years of hiding, I tried to build my next house, my next wall. Learning from the first lesson I chose a stronger medium to construct this one from. As a good little piggy, I chose wood. The attempts that had destroyed my previous home would not work against this one, it and I were stronger now. Happy in my loneliness nothing was going to pull down my walls. However, a house of wood is nothing against the flaming heat of a well-lit fire. My enemies were back, and as they had before they knew exactly how to bring down my hardened walls. They did not have fire themselves; they had been taught it from somewhere. As it turned out, the same people that had given me the gift of fire had given it them, through no fault of their own except ignorance they gave the lesson to my enemies' family, not knowing it would come back on me. When your house burns down it takes your self-worth with it. homeless and hopeless I could not turn to my family; they had caused this mess and yet strangely I felt that I did not deserve their shelter. I had lost my second home; all my walls were gone.

After many years wandering I made one last attempt to build my house. A third house for a third pig. Brick was my material of choice. Made in fire and strong enough not to be pulled down my house reflected myself. Stood alone it gave me confidence that now I was safe. However, with strong walls come those people that want to hide inside. Those people that like you had been before lacked the confidence to build their own home. And so, I shared my strength, and with it I gave them the confidence to build their own walls. My lessons were a little too good though, and once I had taught them all they needed they left my walls and constructed their own without me. Abandoned and once again alone, I learned the one last lesson, as they exited my world, they left the door open behind them and this let anyone that wanted to, just waltz in. with strong walls and an open door the thing that leaves with them as they go is self-respect. Now I had strong walls and no respect, so I let anyone pass through, however, not to let them leave again I pushed them away. Choosing to be alone. I lived a good life, I found purpose and yet my walls became a prison, and so, I pulled them down from inside, freeing myself from their confines.

Without my walls I found my new family, quickly I built my new walls, stronger than before stone and mortar, I had learned my lessons from before, I was careful not to let anyone know how I built my walls and yet without self-belief, self-worth, and self-respect my walls became a prison for those around me, I was safe however I failed to make them feel safe to. It wasn't my enemies that taught me how to build high walls it was my friends and family, it was the people I cared about that showed me their importance, but it was the people that I loved that showed me that my walls are not a good thing, my walls are the prison to another's freedom and so even my strong stone walls, my mighty house began to crumble. Now I live my life, waiting to build my final house, one that cannot be torn down, that does not burn, that cannot be abandoned or be a prison for another, a house, a wall just big enough for me.

Now I wait until I can build my final house, my house of dirt.

The Long road

My bag was packed, my boots tight, and my coat hung by the door, I was ready to go, ready to go on my biggest adventure. I had been getting ready for this one for a while now, saying my goodbyes in my own way, preparing everything around the home for when I was gone. I was ready. I put my coat on and slid my bag over my shoulder and opened the door. The sunlight warmed my face as I stepped outside and I took a moment to close my eyes, tilt my face towards its warming glow and bask in rays, with a deep breath I smelled all the flowers in the garden, an essence of spring filled my nostrils and brought my back down to earth. I was ready, today was the perfect day to begin my adventure and with that I took my first step out of the gate.

As I began to walk along the street, past the various cars and vans that parked along the roadside, another traveler stepped out beside me. He looked as though he too was about to set off on his own adventure. I tried my best to ignore him, I knew it was rude not to acknowledge him, but I had been planning this journey for a while now and I had always planned it to be something I did alone. However, as we both walked down the road, now side by side and in the same stride, I felt the uncomfortable need to say something, maybe if I broke the silence, I could find which way this new traveler was going and plan a new route accordingly.

"Beautiful day, isn't it?" He said before I could get a word out.

"It is," I replied.

"The perfect day to go on an adventure."

"Yes," is all I could muster in response.

My attempt to start an awkward conversation had failed in an instant, somehow, not speaking first had made the situation worse and now I could not find a way to make this new traveler go. I looked at him for the first time, a proper look at least, not just a sidewards glance. He was adorned in much the same outfit as I, albeit a little more monochromatic. My outfit of choice had been blue jeans, brown hiking boots and an orange coat with a red and grey bag. His choice on the other hand was black, black jeans, black boot, black coat, and an all-black bag. This gave me a moment of levity as it was almost like I was.

"Talking to your shadow?" he said as though he had read my thoughts.

"It's the all-black thing," I said, trying to justify my thoughts to him.

"I get that," he replied with a smile.

We walked on a little further in silence until we reached a fork in the road. The road to the left looked smooth but long, to the right the road seemed to give way to cobbles and after that what could only be described as jagged rocks. I looked down both roads trying to decide which way to go, my adventure had no set destination, so I didn't care where each path led.

"So which way are you going?" my new companion asked. "Left, or right?"

The choice seemed easy enough I could take the smooth road, get to wherever it led and be able to carry on but as I looked at the other traveler, he seemed to be edging that way and so I chose the right path, the cobbled path.

"Think I'll head this way," I told him and I began to walk away.

"Okay," he replied with a smile.

With that I was alone once more. The cobbled path slowed my progress and as the stones became rocks and the cobbles replaced with jagged edges my progress all but stopped. Each step had to be carefully planned, carefully thought through before I could take another step. My adventure had already begun with a trial. I knew I needed to persevere, I had planned this little adventure of mine for so long and nothing was going to stop me. By the time I reached the other end of the road

I was met with a cheery hello. My old companion had arrived at that exact same moment, his longer road had led him to the same place, and although his route was considerably longer, we arrived at the same destination at the same time.

"Who would have guessed it?" he asked.

We continued down the road in silence for a little while, both hoping the other would break the silence but neither of us did. We strolled together, the sun on our backs, like two old friends, no need for words, just enjoying the walk together. It was then I realized that the silence was no longer awkward. I wanted to comment on it but before I found the words, we reached another fork.

"Left, or right?" he asked me again.

I looked down each road, the path to the left disappeared int a thicket of trees whilst the path to the right seemed clear.

"I am enjoying the stroll," I said to him. "I think I shall take the right path again."

"Okay," he replied and with a skip in his step he set off towards the tree line.

My path was a long one, full of twists and turns, the road was decent, the walking simple enough, it was just that without my companion to walk beside me it did seem that the walk was taking longer than it should. Twist after twist, turn after turn, I began to regret my choice, my route was boring. The sun set and night fell upon me, so I quickly set up my camp and rested for the night. By the next morning I was refreshed and rearing to go. Another day passed, then another, and another. The road seemed to lead nowhere, yet it was this emptiness that drove me to want to set out on the adventure, and so, spurred on by this, I set off one final day along this path. By the end of the fifth day, as the sun began to set, I saw a faint light in the distance. Knowing that it might be the first sign of civilization that I had seen in nearly a week I pressed on. As I arrived at the light, a campfire before two tents I heard a familiar voice.

"What took you so long? I have been here for days."

My old companion was back, and I was filled with joy because I was not alone anymore. We sat together into the night in silence before retiring to the tents for a few hours before we set off once more. There was so much I wanted to say, and yet I still could not find the words, instead we strolled on together in our usual voiceless manner. Instead, I tried to let my attentions drift off elsewhere, I looked out over the fields, marveling at how rich and vibrant the colours were. I watched as the birds flew overhead chirping out a beautiful melody that I could feel myself humming along to. I felt a cool breeze wash over my face causing the hairs to stand on end and my skin to tingle.

Everything was perfect and I knew I was right to come on my adventure.

Sensing my pleasure my companion stopped walking for a moment and I had to take a step back to be in line with him.

"Why have we stopped?" I asked.

"So that you can realise the simple truth," He replied.

"What truth?"

"That the grass was just as green yesterday, that the birds sand the same songs a week ago and that every breeze you have ever felt on you face was like a lovers kiss."

I didn't know what to say to him. I was sure I hadn't said what I was thinking and yet again he seemed to know how to respond.

"Now come along," he said and began walking once more.

I had to jog the first couple of steps to catch up with him, however I was soon by his side once more.

We didn't talk after that. The day ended in silence and a new one started in silence. Even the birds had stopped singing as we strolled along, ever closer to our destination, although I still did not know where I was heading.

By the time we reached the next fork I just wanted to get away from my companion for a little while, somehow, he had found a way to remove all the joy from our walk and I just wanted to get some of the magic that I had felt back. So, when It came time to choose, I took the right path without looking at what the other might have in store for me. I strolled off without a word, looking up into the sky, hoping to find the birds there once more. With the skies empty I looked down to the floor, the grass was all gone, just the dull grey of concrete all around.

"The wind," I called to myself. Yet as I closed my eyes to allow the breeze to kiss my face once more, the whole world seemed to stop around me, no wind, no breeze. I tried to run forward, hoping that I would create a breeze on my face but instead, I was just met with a sense of emptiness. Defeated I continued along the road until I reached the other end where my travelling partner arrived in unison.

We walked together in silence once more, I wanted to talk, wanted to apologise but found no words on my tongue. My companion didn't seem that interested either, instead he walked beside me, eyes forward, trudging along to our destination.

As we reached the final fork in the road, we noticed this one was a little different. Neither direction seemed to curve, twist, raise or dip, the just went on.

"Let me guess," my companion said. "You intend to take the right path once more."

Both paths looked identical to me. If I was to spin on the spot and lose my bearings, I could easily confuse one path with the other.

"Which one are you taking?" I asked, hoping that he would finally allow me to continue along with him. I hoped for a chance to apologise, to try and continue this adventure with him rather than alone as I had originally intended.

"Neither," he replied.

His simple and short answer caught me off guard and before I could think of what else to say, my companion had disappeared back along the path that we had come down. Furthermore, the path seemed to vanish just as quick as he had.

I know found myself stood in the centre of a long unwinding road, no way to get back to where I had been, no way back to where it had all begun, now I had two choices, and both meant moving on. I stood there for what felt like an age, trying to find something different between them, would one path give me more joy, would the birds return, and the breeze kiss my face. Neither path gave me any clues, neither path looked to be the right way.

I closed my eyes and spun around until I was so dizzy that I fell to the floor, as the back of my head collided with a stone, I heard a whisper, as though from a distant memory.

"The simple truth."

And with that I picked myself up, dusted myself off, and with eyes closed I took my first step back into the breeze.

The affair

He had not always felt this way; he was a loving and trusting man. He loved his wife with all of his heart and although he had times when he would forget to show it, or take that she was with him for granted it did not mean that she did not know it or that she in any way felt less about him than he did her.

Their busy lives meant that they did not get to spend as much time together as either of them would have liked but they always tried to make up for it when they could. Candle lit dinners, running each other baths after a long day. Feeding each other strawberries, or chocolates and sweets that they took from the children's cupboard. They sat together, watched films and television series that the other one wanted and shared a laugh together when they cuddled up in bed every night. So, Alan found himself a little confused about how he was feeling now. His problems had started, as so many do, with a dream. It wasn't a bad dream, well not at first. He dreamt of him and his children on holiday together, they were looking in the shops for some little trinkets to mark the occasion when they stumbled across a little curiosity shop. The kind of shop that had all the same junk outside as every other shop but theirs was that little bit different. The usual cheap plastic toys were made of wood, the dolls looked hand made. And so, at the behest of his children they went inside. The shop was laid out over multiple floors each one a little smaller than the last. As they reached the top floor however, they were met by a locked door. Alan peered through the gap at the edge of the door and could see another opening. The showed his eldest and they decided to try to find another way around.

Another door appeared, not as though by magic but more of one of those feelings that they had somehow just missed it before and as they walked through the entered the locked room. The room was empty apart from a very small and very narrow set of stairs in the corner. The gap was too small for Alan and yet he decided to try anyway. Getting stuck half way he called to the children for help, and yet he received none. Forcing himself out of the gap he fell back into the room and saw his children sitting on a bench, that had not been there before and there was two other people laid out in the centre of the room. One was a man that Alan had no recollection of, a very plain man, short hair, smartly dressed and thinly built, all the features that would not describe himself. The man was on his back, his head slightly raised though. His knees however were raised to form a backrest for the other person. Alan's wife Isabelle. She was sat against his legs, her lower body straight out away from him. her phone in hand she just sat there without a care in the world. Angrily Alan caught her eye by frantically waving at her. Too polite to shout as this would disturb the man in the room.

As Isabelle rose to her feet her frustration was clear for Alan to see. She walked over to him, silently and yet aggressively mouthing one word;

"What?"

Alan took her hand and strolled through the door that had been locked before and somehow found himself and his wife inside his childhood kitchen.

"What do you mean what?" he barked at her gesturing towards the man in the other room. However, Isabelle gave him no reply.

"You just sit there with another man right in front of me? Why would you do that?"

"Well, I wouldn't want to lay there with you now, would I?" her response caused him to step back in confused silence which gave her the opportunity to continue, "Why would I? lying next to you makes me feel sick," and with that she turned her back on her husband and started to walk away. This was the moment that Alan awoke from his dream, its vivid imagery lasting beyond the moment that the confusion lifted and he found himself in his bed, Isabelle peacefully sleeping beside him. he rolled over and picked up his phone to check the time.

05:35

Was displayed in the top corner. With only twenty-five minutes until his alarm would sound, he decided that the best course of action was to just get up early and start his day.

Days had passed since the night of the dream and yet, for some reason, Alan could not get it out of his mind. He had told Isabelle about it the next day and she had given him a reassuring hug before he left for work that day. Yet, as the days rolled on and he found himself sat in a quiet room or alone on the bus his mind would creep back to the feeling that something wasn't right. He knew that he was being stupid, Isabelle loved him and would never do that, she would never cheat, never stray he was sure of it. however, if you have ever had an idea stuck in your head for any length of time the one thing that your mind does well, as evil as it can be, is to find evidence that what you are thinking is correct. For Alan this started after a few nights when Isabelle was sat on the sofa with him watching one of those shows that she had no interest in but watched for him. this time seemed a little different. Totally engrossed in the show Alan hadn't noticed the phone in her hand, he was somewhat unaware of her presence at all until he heard he laughing at a part of the show that was in no way funny. He drew his attention to her and saw the phone in her hand.

"What's so funny?" he asked her.

"Oh nothing, just a message from Sharon," Sharon was her oldest friend and the two of them only really communicated through phone messages, so this was normal to him, he turned back to the screen as she laughed again and again. His focus was gone from the show and he turned back to her, catching a glimpse of the phone as he did, messenger as usual but the picture on the conversation was a little different.

"Sharon got a new picture," he said half as a question half statement.

"What, oh, yeah," Isabelle replied and with that the conversation was over and the phone went away. This was the first piece of evidence that Alan had that something was wrong.

After this, the proof came flooding back to him. every time that she had failed to message her when she said that she would. The change in her style on the days that they were not together. Messages from old friends and colleagues from her new job that she had never really spoke about before. Alan was on edge, he started to focus on what was wrong, had he neglected her and now she was looking for comfort from anywhere that she could find it.

He knew that he had to change and so he waited for her to get home from work. She worked late and had a long commute and so he set about with his plans to sweep her off of her feet as she walked in. She had just finished work, he knew that which meant that he had a good forty minutes to prepare a little supper, set out the candles, get changed into her favourite outfit that he owned and so he frantically gathered everything together to set up his impromptu date. However, within ten minutes the back gate opened and Isabelle strolled in. she was out of her work uniform wearing a nice summer top under her coat and was home far too early.

"How did you get back so quick," Alan asked with an unintentional hint of anger due to the fact that his carefully thought-out plan was ruined.

"A couple of us got a lift," she said a little taken aback by the tone of his voice "I wanted to get home to you," she carried on but Alan did not hear that part, or if he did, chose to ignore it. he stomped over to the oven and switched it off, pushed the candles back into the drawer and marched off upstairs to put the clothes away. Isabelle followed him upstairs and got changed for bed, slid in behind him, rolled over and went to sleep.

To Alan the story played out a little different. In his mind she had left out of uniform because she wasn't going to work. The lift home was from whomever she was spending the evening with. probably the same person that she had been messaging a few nights earlier when she had said it was Sharon. To him this was evidence that she was having an affair, and so, he decided that he would prove it, he would find all the evidence that she was cheating and would present it to her as he walked out the door and took the kids with him. the first thing he needed to do was find the name of the man that she was with, and so every time she took out her phone to answer a message, he would try to glance at whom she was corresponding with. Then after he spotted a name, he would find a way to bring it up in conversation. There was one name that stood out though, Bradley, whenever he asked about Bradley, she would find an excuse to change the conversation. Avoiding any explanation as to who this man was and so, Alan decided that this must be him. he started looking on Isabelle's social media accounts looking for a Bradley or Brad, however he found none.

"Probably not got him on here just in case I looked," he growled to himself as he finished looking through the list. With no other way to find him, he had to resort to the one thing that he said he would never do. He looked at her phone, waiting for her to fall asleep that night he placed the finger print scanner against each finger in turn until he heard the phone unlock. Quickly he checked the messages for Bradley's name and when he found it, he read the last message that she had sent to him. this was enough.

I'll meet you outside White Lion at 2 tomorrow.

That was it the proof that he needed, he knew a time and place that she was meeting him and he would be there. The next morning, he got up as usual, made the children breakfast and got dressed for work, he set out at the normal time, promptly at eight and set off in the usual direction, however, once he had rounded the corner and was not going to be seen he called into work to tell his manager that he wasn't going to be able to make it.

"My son has taken ill and Isabelle isn't available to take him to the doctors,"

A simple little lie, and he had felt the twinge of guilt for it, that and using his son's health as an excuse. However, it was important and he knew it, the only problem now was that he had six hours to wait for the meet. He walked to the white lion and found a little coffee bar across the way, one of those old converted houses where the upstairs becomes a seating area. He ordered a coffee and a carrot cake and went up to find a seat overlooking the entrance to the White Lion. Six hours he sat there, drinking more coffee than one man should have in a week let alone one day. Six hours he waited, replaying his entire relationship over in his head, trying to figure out what he had done wrong, how he had driven her to cheat on him. by the time two o'clock rolled around he was furious, angry at every man that walked within thirty feet of the Pub's door. About ten past two he saw Isabelle arrive, she wasted no time walking over to one of the men hanging around outside the door, he greeted her with a box, he was giving her a present and then she flung her arms around him, the box in her hand and with a huge smile on her face she started to head back the way that she came. Bradley sat back down outside the pub to finish what was left of his afternoon pint before he walked off in the opposite direction to Isabelle.

Alan was furious, so much so that he walked out of the café without paying for his last drink. He stormed across the road through oncoming cars and as Bradley walked far enough away that he could not see him he started to run after him. as he rounded the corner, he saw Bradley entering a house a few doors down. Alan's blood was boiling, he knew what needed to be done now. Taking the kids was not punishment enough. He grabbed a loose brick off the wall next to him and charged to the door before it could close. Crashing through the door behind Bradley he swung the brick with all his might, catching Bradley on the temple. Bradley collapsed to the floor and stopped moving instantly. Seeing what he had done, Alan threw down the brick and fled back out of the open door and down the road. He had meant to kill him, however the actual act left him with a feeling of guilt that he had not expected.

"He's been sleeping with my wife," he told himself, "He deserved it," his justification was weak but was enough to keep him focussed. He set off home but had arrived too early, he was meant to be at work and so, he sat at the end of the road watching his watch tick on, waiting for the time he was meant to be home.

At five o'clock, a few minutes earlier than he would normally arrive home he walked into the house. He was expecting to find the children at the table, eating their dinner but they were not there. Instead, he walked in to a trail of rose petal's leading towards the stairs, following the trail towards the bedroom his anger morphed into confusion, he pushed open the door to find his wife, laying across the bed in some new lingerie, a scented candle burning on the bedside table and more white rose petals surrounding the box that he had seen her take from Bradley. The box was open and he could see that inside was an antique pocket watch, similar to one his grandfather had owned.

"I'm sorry that I have been a little different around you recently," she said in a soft tone as he walked into the room. "I have not been feeling myself."

Alan was stunned at the sight of her, waiting on the bed for him. he struggled to find the words to say, not sure what he was thinking, eventually landing on;

"The kids?"

"They are at your mothers, and I have taken the night off work so that we can reconnect," she moved towards him and took him by the hand.

"I thought you were having an affair?" he blurted out, tears starting to form in the corner of his eyes. "Bradley?" he said through a held back whimper.

"Bradley sold me the watch, I knew that you always wanted to get one, to remind you of your grandad and when I saw it, I knew I had to get it. it was supposed to be a birthday present; I was going to give it to you next month but with how you have been feeling recently I thought I should give it to you now."

Alan burst into tears as she gave him the watch and tried to lean forward to kiss him

"You don't understand, I thought you was meeting him to sleep with him," he said as he collapsed to the floor, "I followed you there and saw you hug him. I watched you leave and followed him home. I thought you were cheating on me with him, that you were going to leave me, I thought that you were sleeping with him and so I killed him."

Fear of the dark

"It is not the dark that frightens me, nor is it the monsters that lay under my bed or peer out of the wardrobe when I close my eyes. It's the silence.

When there is nothing else around, no sounds, no birds, everyone else is fast asleep as they should be; this is the moments I fear most. I can't hide from them forever, a day or two at most and then my body gives up and succumbs to the silence. I know there is nothing there, nothing between us and yet I cannot let myself go from the quiets deafening grasp. Have you ever found yourself somewhere so devoid of sound that you can hear your heart beat, you blood course through your veins? This is when they come.

A whisper at first, then with each passing iteration they get louder and louder until you are no longer engulfed in silence, but rather, smothered by their taunts, suffocated by their irrefutable and yet flawed logic. The daemons of my loathing, tormenting and torturing me for their own sick amusement.

By the time the sun rises, the birds begin their morning chorus, and life begins back up around me, I find myself so beguiled by their words that for the next day I cannot forget their message and before it has had chance to escape my ears it is replaced by the eerie countdown of yet another silence."

It was not the first time Samuel had found himself discussing the darkness, trying to tell someone, anyone that could understand what was happening to him. Unfortunately, this was not the audience that was going to help. The first pidgeon cocked its head to the side, one eye darting about as though looking him over. A second hopped across to his feet, searching for some kind of leftover, a crumb that it could make its own. They weren't being talkative, their lack of cooperation reminding Samuel that he had been here before so many times.

He clung onto the edge of the bridge and leant over as far as his reach and balance would allow.

"From this height I may actually survive."

He stepped back away from the edge of the ledge, his heart pounding and his stomach turning as he thought of himself a coward.

"Once more," he said as he pulled his coat up around his face and sauntered back off the bridge.

With a deep breath and a sigh, he walked to work and as he reached the front door of the office, his office, he sighed once more and headed inside. The next nine hours passed without so much as a thought of the bridge. This wasn't the first time he had found himself here and he was sure it would not be the last.

Another two weeks had passed before Samuel found himself once again standing on the tip of a ledge. This time it was the platform of the local train station. He looked around for someone to talk to and yet there wasn't even a single bird in the sky.

"Typical," he mumbled to himself. "Bad enough when no one replies, what's the point when no one is even here to listen?"

"It is not the dark that frightens me," he began, speaking to nothing in particular. When he had finished, he stepped onto the track and waited for the next train. Silence washed over him and he attempted to embrace it.

"Failure," the voice chimed in. "Look."

He opened his eyes and felt them drawn to the floor, the track he had stood on was incomplete, out of service.

"Probably for the best," he mumbled to himself as he stepped back onto the platform and proceeded out of the gate.

Samuel lived his life like this, too scared to stop moving, terrified what his daemons would say to him when the world stood still. Over the years he tried everything to dull the noise, working until he dropped, fanaticizing about being able to one day take that extra step; not to over think his every thought and action and finally be able to let go. So, when he stepped out into the road that day without noticing the speeding car and was run down and as the darkness finally came for him, an absolute silence that he no longer needed to fear no one was more shocked than he was that a tear trickled down his face.

He didn't want to go.

Trouble in Auldrun

The streets were particularly dark this evening, a fact that Michael was happy about. The main pedestrian walkway through the town was the sort of place one wanted to slip through unnoticed.

The November air was cold as it was every night. The kind of bitter cold that scraped and scratched your throat as it tore its way down into your lungs. Michael dropped his chin down to his chest and walked peering through his eyebrows, his thick winter coat offered some protection from the weather however he hated covering his face no matter how cold it got. The only protection he had was the unkempt beard that had been allowed to grow over the past few days.

As he walked through the high street, he marvelled at all the closed down shops, for sale signs, and boarded windows that littered this once beautiful and picturesque thoroughfare. The newsagent that had given him his first job, gone; replaced by an electric cigarette store. The shoe shop that his mother had bought his school shoes was now a greasy Chinese takeaway, complete with dirty windows, red lights, and lucky waving cat. Even the pub that he managed to buy his first pint in at the tender age of fourteen was now a charity shop. The only thing worse than the for-sale signs was that the only businesses that seemed to be successful were tanning salons and nail parlours. He had always wondered what "other" services they offered to keep their doors open on such a rundown and desolate street. However, he could never pluck up the courage to investigate.

The only thing worse than the sights of the old town were the sounds and smells. The entire street carried a musk of marijuana, a smell Michael hated with every fibre of his being. Although it did manage to hide the underlying stench of stale beer and piss that oozed out of every boarded shop front. It was so disgusting that even the homeless contingent would avoid settling down on this street. Then there were the sounds. A chorus of monotonous thumps as everyone tried to drown out their neighbours' noise pollution even though every song sounded exactly the same to him. This "music" was accompanied by a symphony of car alarms and police sirens that gave Auldrun its own unique, albeit undesirable, soundtrack.

With his head down and his hands tucked firmly in his pockets he marched home. The walk was not far, a little under a half mile, but here it seemed to be a lot further. He wanted to get back, travel unnoticed, escape. Each step echoed off the walls either side of him which made it sound as though the streets were actually busy.

As he reached the end of the pedestrian area his path was flanked by two pubs. The blue stag, a boiler that had more in kin with a smackheads den than a public house, and the Auldrun arms, an institution that prided itself of its civil war heritage even though most of the punters could hardly spell civil... Or war. This was the part he dreaded the most, he wasn't sure of the time but knew it had to be near closing time and if he was as unlucky as he usually was, he would walk between them at kicking out time. A time when two tribes of drunk Neanderthals would stumble into the street, hurl illegible abuse at one another before the inevitable dust up that concluded most nights in town. If that happened the police would soon arrive and everyone, even a passer-by would be corralled and questioned and that was the last thing that he wanted. He had made it to the door when the thunderous wave emanated from the stag as its door swung open and three young ladies stumbled out. One barely looked old enough to drink, a little hypocritical from a man that was served at fourteen, but now he just looked at her and wondered what her parents were thinking. The second was well dressed, smart, suited like she worked for a fortune 500 company and stopped off for a quiet one in her way home, an unlikely pairing anywhere, never mind here. The final lady was, as he could tell now, certainly not young. Mid-fifties at least and yet she wore less clothing than the others in the misguided hope that it would make herself look younger. Instead, her ass high skirt and decorative belt that was made of more material than the skirt it adorned, thigh high red leather boots, and a cropped top that seemed to be struggling to hang on, made her look more like a lady of the night than a young lass on a night out.

"Oi, what you looking at?" The teenager asked in a slurred tone.

Michael buried his face in his collar and walked on.

"She asked you a question," the older one chimed in. "See something you like?"

This was not what he wanted to happen, not tonight, so he picked up his pace a little.

"Too good for us," the well-dressed one added.

"For you maybe," the teenager laughed.

This seemed to make Michael instantly forgettable as the three women argued and laughed at each other in their way to find some greasy food, or other bad decision. Alone again Michael tried to keep up his new pace but the fear that someone else might step outside and engage him weighed heavily and he decided to swing up one of the connecting side streets. This led into the main road and was well lit, two things that he was hoping to avoid. However, needs must and so he decided that he had better chance it.

The main road wasn't a long one, barely two hundred yards to his front door. A solid wall on one side and a row of houses on the other. The houses were all tucked behind walls and large bushes as the owners tried to drown out some of the noise caused by all the traffic that raced along the road in the day. Tonight though, seemed uncharacteristically quiet. He took the opportunity to get across the road and disappeared in the shadowy darkness caused by a row of parked cars. He was barely a hundred and fifty yards from his front door. A few more moments and he would be home. He started counting the neighbour's doors, counting down to the safety of his own door.

"Five."

The house had a beautiful garden, set out like a Parisian Cafe.

"Four."

A stark contrast, empty yard, bland curtains, and cracked paint on both the gate and door.

"Three."

A large unkempt hedge his most of this house.

"Two."

Bins dumped in the front, a for sale signs still hanging over the gate even though the house sold a year ago.

"One."

The final house and garden, a perfect display of wild flowers, decorative pottery, and perfectly clean white stone walkways. Michael always loved seeing this garden before he turned into his own. He was jealous of how beautiful they could make it look; nothing he tried to grow ever survived. He almost forgot himself, allowing his pace to slow to a crawl as he took in the magnificence of his neighbour's handy work. Until the night air was suddenly awash with blue and red lights and the quiet stillness came crashing to an end as a multitude of sirens rattled off the walls in a deafening display.

He dropped to the floor, rolled himself over to the nearest car and leant against the wheel; waiting for the police cars to pass. He couldn't risk being stopped by them, not this close to home. The night sky flashed like a bonfire display for quite some time after the sirens died away, however, the calmness of the night did finally return. Michael looked at his front door for a while, he could get in that way but the creaking could wake his wife, the inside was as dark as the outside so he knew she would be asleep and therefore better to circle around the back.

He decided to run this last stretch, the police were out and people would be curtain twitching soon and he did not want to be seen, as he ran up the side of his house he stepped into a large puddle and an icy blast of water shot up his leg causing him to let out a little shriek. He reached his gate, opened it carefully and slid into his back yard. Half of his yard was lit by a nearby street light but the portion behind the gate and the path to the back door were shrouded in darkness. He couldn't go inside like this; he was a mess. He took his jacket off and laid it on the floor by his feet. He kicked off his dry shoe and forced the wet one off and discarded them inside his jacket, then he peeled off his socks, followed by his shirt, trousers and finally his boxers. The night air was freezing, his entire body began to shiver and shake. He quickly grabbed his clothes together and stepped into the light of the street lamp so that he could place the pile into the bin. He used some of the contents from inside to cover the pile and closed the lid before retreating back into the dark praying that he had not been seen. He wasn't carrying a phone key or wallet so he had nothing to gather as he went inside and immediately turned into the bathroom that was beside the back door.

Jumping into the shower to wash away the evenings grime he finally felt warm and was enjoying the hot jets a little too much. He scrubbed himself clean, washed his hair and then his body one more time. he didn't want to get out of the water but he knew that he must. He grabbed a towel off the back of the door and wrapped it around his waist before leaning back over the bath to turn the shower off. A quick dry and then he was ready to head upstairs to bed. He hung the towel back on the door and strolled through the house naked. He knew the layout and was able to navigate his way upstairs without incident. He entered the bedroom and quietly slid into bed beside his wife.

He had made it in without disturbing her, he closed his eyes and replayed the evening back to himself.

"Good night?" his wife asked.

"Yes," he replied, a little smile breaking its way across his face.

"Get up to anything?"

"Nothing too bad," he replied.

"That's nice," she said.

Michael could hear in her voice that she was drifting off once more and so he lay in silence waiting for to fall back asleep. Once he was sure she was gone, he grabbed his phone off the bedside table.

BREAKING NEWS

The notification from a local news group pinged onto the screen. Michael double clicked it and waited for it to load up. He only needed the headline to know what was happening.

THREE DEAD IN AULDRUN DRUG DEN, POLICE HAVE NO LEADS

Michael put his phone back down, smiled at his handy work and drifted off to a deep and comfortable sleep.

The Game

The bullet slid into the chamber with a resounding clunk. Stephen was shocked at just how loud it seemed against the quiet backdrop of the cold winter night. The icy metal still left a chill on his fingers as he pushed the wheel of his Ruger revolver closed. He knew the gun was new but couldn't help but feel like a cowboy holding his six shooter, however, with only a single bullet, it felt more like he was about to play Russian roulette rather than take part in a duel. He wrapped the fingers of his left hand around the grip and felt the weight of the weapon in his hand, trying to get comfortable holding it. He had never held a gun before and thought that it was probably something that he was supposed to do before he tried firing it for the first time.

When he was finally comfortable with the gun in his hand he walked over to his motorcycle, a small 100cc motocross bike, that looked as though it had been dropped a few too many times in its life to still run properly, and yet, it somehow managed to chug on. He couldn't help but be impressed by its build quality, not that that would help him now. He climbed atop the bike with his fingers still firmly wrapped around his gun and he took the throttle in his free hand and gave it a few twists. Listening to the engine roar to life he had almost forgotten why he was here; what it was he was about to do. However, he was soon brought crashing back down to reality as a large man walked over to him with a leather strap in his hands.

Stephen felt the man was obviously a biker, with his long grey hair and matching beard, that contained whisps of his original auburn, black jeans that had started to tear through years of excessive use, black leather vest Jacket, and Metallica t-shirt. He found himself impressed that he could stand out here on this cold night without a coat or a care. He watched as, without a word the grey-haired biker man started to tie Stephens' hand to the throttle. He knew this was going to happen but hadn't anticipated the dread that would wash over him as his hand was strapped down.

"You need to hear the rules again?" the biker asked in his deep, gravelly voice.

Stephen started to reply; however, the man didn't wait for his response.

"It's simple," he huffed in a voice that told Stephen that this wasn't the first time he had explained the rules over to someone. "You got to stay above 30 at all times." The lazy tone did nothing to help Stephen's anxiety, that was beginning to build with each passing minute.

"You can put the gun away to use the clutch, but I wouldn't recommend it," he continued, in an unnerving monotone that was beginning to impress Stephen in exactly the same measure as it was causing him to panic.

"And don't drop the fucking gun on the street, because I'm not looking for it for you," the sarcastic tone in which he said these last words made Stephen chuckle under his breath, but he knew this guy was serious.

"Other than that," he continued. "Wait for the green light." with that he walked off back into the dark.

Stephen could feel his arms starting to shake. He tried to convince himself that it was down to the cold and not that he was frightened, but he was lying to himself. He was aware that this was a bad idea, but he needed the money, win or lose, he knew he would at least earn enough to pay for his son's medical bills. In fact, if he won a couple of times, he might earn enough to get himself out of debt altogether. He watched as the first red light filled the night with its bright and ominous glow and even though it was only a few seconds before the amber light took its place, to him, those few seconds felt like a lifetime.

As the amber light filled the darkness, he pulled the clutch with the grip of the gun, kicked the bike into first and gave the throttle a quick twist as though he was trying to wake the machine up for work. As the green light took its turn, he released the clutch and the bike jumped to life like a startled horse. The small engine soon began to rev, forcing Stephen to begin to shift through the gears, Second, then third and quickly into fourth. The stretch of road was barely two miles long, without knowing his speed and remembering that he had to remain above thirty, he continued to accelerate until he noticed the other bike coming towards him. He soon realised that the other bike was moving at a much slower speed than he was travelling, and Stephen was sure that this meant that his opponent had done this before.

With even less resolve than he had setting off, Stephen raised his left hand and stretched the gun out as far as he could. The wind raced down the sleeve of his Jacket and it wasn't more than a few seconds before his whole forearm had gone numb, but still he rode. The silhouette of the other rider grew with each passing second and it wasn't long before Stephen could see he too had his arm stretched straight out. He pulled his finger a little tighter on the trigger, a feat that the numbness was making unnecessarily difficult, squeezing until he felt it push against him and he held it there.

As the two men rode passed each other there was a loud crack as both men pulled their triggers and fired their weapons in unison. Stephen felt himself wobble as the gun jolted back in his hand, but he was quickly able to compose himself. He was fine. The other guy had missed him. He wanted to look back, but he was still in shock after what he had just done that his body was too tense to turn.

"I… I…I killed him," he muttered under his laboured breath. "I did it."

He rode ever closer to the other end of the road where he saw another man waiting for him. This one also resembled a biker, he thought, however this one was wearing a big winter coat, with the almost uniform heavily worn black jeans and huge Newrock boots. From afar he looked much younger than the other guy, his hair had virtually no visible grey throughout the short black strands and yet as he approached, the lines on his face gave the impression that he was at least in his seventies. Stephen let the bike slow down through the gears as he approached the man and stopped a few feet shy of the hastily painted line that he realised was probably on the other end of the road just this was the first time he had noticed it.

"Hurry over," the man in the coat shouted to him. He spoke with a deep middle American accent, like he was in one of those old cowboy movies. "I said, hurry!" he shouted again, only this time making him aware that it was an order and not a suggestion. Stephen hopped off the bike and pushed it over.

"Turn it around, you got to go again," he pointed back down the road from where Stephen had just come. "You boys got to keep going, got to go until one of you loses."

Stephen's heart felt like it had just fallen to his feet, he hadn't won, he was fine, but so was the other guy. He climbed back on the bike and turned it to face down the road again and held out his gun ready for another bullet. The man loaded another single bullet into the wheel and closed it ready to fire and as soon as that was done, he walked away leaving Stephen to stare at the lights waiting, once more, for them to go green.

The next lap went almost exactly the same as the first, accelerating too quickly, holding the gun outstretched for too long and missing the shot as the two men passed. Lap three was the same again, as was laps four and five, and Stephen was beginning to feel that it would never end, however, by the time he had completed his seventh lap he was beginning to get used to the weight of the gun and he felt that his shots were at least coming close to hitting their target, and with this new sense of confidence he rode out again, also, over the last few attempts he had stopped raising his hand so early, his arm wasn't getting numb anymore and he was able to hold the gun steady for longer.

As the two men passed each other for the eighth time Stephen heard the sound of his opponents' gun fire, but he hadn't pulled the trigger of his own. He rode back, confused, he was confident that this time would have been the one, but he hadn't even taken the shot. Frustrated he pulled up to the line and held his gun out for another bullet, he saw his old friend with the big beard and no coat staring at him.

"Come on," Stephen heard himself shouting. "Give me the fucking bullet."

However, the man just stared at him. He impatiently slammed the gun down on the gas tank and began sorting it for the next run, it wasn't until he picked the gun back up that he noticed that it was wet, and that it was covered in a dark liquid, almost as black as tar. As the crimson light filled the nights sky once more, he realised, the gun was covered in blood. His blood.

The darkness

I want to explain to you the darkness. But I don't know if I can. Not because I don't have the words, no, the words are easy. It's not because I don't know how it makes me feel, I do, I most certainly know how I feel and the words to best express it. the problem is, in order to really explain the darkness, I have to open up to you, open up in a way that I never have before. Now the first thing that I must make clear is that the darkness isn't the actions that I take, but rather the thoughts that my mind jumps to. It is the dark recess in the back of my mind that always jumps to the wrong conclusions. Some might see it as trust issues, other as paranoia but the simple fact is that they are there, they are always there and they infect my mind constantly.

Now the darkness is not about any one person, and it doesn't stop me from making connections, from falling in love or making friends, it doesn't stop me from trusting people either, what it does do is flood my mind with scenarios and take the world around me to make sense of them. I do not think that every time I am apart from the one that I love that she is being unfaithful, that would be too simple for the cruelty of the darkness, no, what it does is give me the image of her with another man, and then show me how they met, how he convinced her to do these things. The darkness shows me my flaws and how I am responsible for her actions. How I drove her away, how I drove her into his arms. However, the darkness isn't done with me there. It shows me how they enjoy all the things that we have enjoyed together and how they laugh together at doing all the things that she will not do with me. Then it takes something trivial, a little detail like her failure to respond to a text or how she doesn't answer the phone as proof that it is right. Even a simple message is dissected to prove the darkness's point.

It is not just this though, the darkness infects more than this. It takes its time with me, shows me ways that everyone is against me, how my job is pushing and pulling those close to me away, how any interaction no matter how innocent will lead to people leaving and distrusting me. I wait patiently for the darkness to finally prove itself right and this itself helps the darkness take a hold. Rationality doesn't have a place in the darkness, the laws of common sense have no sway in the world in which it creates. In order to show you what I mean I will just begin by telling you the times the darkness has taken its time with my mind.

I was at work, and she had finally got a message to sell a piece of furniture that I had asked her to get rid of. Someone was coming to collect it at noon. My lunch break began at ten minutes to twelve and I did what I always did, I walked out and called her. She answered and was just beginning to tell me about her day when I heard a knock at our door over the phone

"I've got to go," she told me and quickly hung up. I knew she hung up so that she could answer the door and make the sale but this is where the darkness has its fun.

"She didn't need to hang up," it began with a whisper, a truth in itself as I would have happily waited on the line to continue our talk, but still, I understood why she hung up.

"Some strange man is in your house," it continued, an easy one to ignore, they were there to but the furniture. Then the fun began.

"What if they aren't, maybe it's some guy from her work coming over because you aren't there," another one I could argue with myself.

"The furniture would still be there," I said to myself, a simple retort to dissuade the darkness's advance.

"He is going to take the furniture," it responded, a response that made no sense.

"Why would he take a piece of furniture just for an excuse to come over?"

"Because she has planned in case you came home," it replied. "You'll walk in and they will just start to remove it through the front door and tell you that he had come over seen it and nipped to fetch some cash after deciding that he wanted it."

The detail the darkness came up with started to take affect at this point and I was convinced to call back, five minutes should have been plenty of time to make a simple transaction. The phone rang through to answer phone, I tried again, to the same result. The darkness had won, the thought was unshakable to me now. An hour later I got a message telling me how she had been sorting other things and this was why she hadn't answered but the thought had festered by that point.

My mind, the darkness, this demon on my shoulder, whatever you want to call it has won, it has caused me to question everything all the time. every phone call, text message, story I have been told. It has defeated me because I can no longer ignore what it is telling me. I trust people, believe in them and yet whenever the darkness wants to take a hold it will and does and I have no way to stop it. When I try the darkness berates me, hounds me with thoughts that I am not good enough, not wanted, and that the world would be a better place without me in it. These are the moments I fear the most. The moments that have given me inside knowledge of what water filling your lungs feels like, the way a rope caresses your skin before the burn as it tightens.

However, I will not lose, I will not give in to the darkness, not today, not ever. The darkness only has strength when you allow yourself to fear it. Only holds sway whilst you fail to understand it. I will turn to the light, my light, to keep the darkness at bay.

Poetry

A letter to my unborn child

I write this letter to you, my son

Knowing that you will never see it.

I write this letter to you, my daughter

Knowing that you will never hear it.

I write this letter to you, my child

Because I need to feel it.

Never will I see your smile,

Hear your laugh or

Comfort you when you cry.

These words are not for you, my child

Because deep down I know that I need it

I need to tell you that I love you

Because I want you to understand

That no matter how brief your life was

You have a permanent place in my mind

I cannot find the words to say

The lightning strike of emotion

The moment that I learned of you

You held my heart, my devotion

I write this letter to you, my son

Because my tears stop me from seeing it.

I write this letter to you, my daughter

My sobs stop me from hearing it.

I write this letter to you, my child

Because I will never stop feeling it.

We will never share a smile,

Make each other laugh or

Share a comforting tear.

These words I share with you, my child

To help my heart to stop grieving.

Silver linings

I look out to a sunless sky

Obscured by the darkest clouds

A rain about to fall upon me

Thunder about to muffle my cries

And yet I can see the silver linings

That will temper my despair

Like the clouds, a world without me

Would be brightened once again

I try to remember being happy

Looking back on older times

But none appear before me

Nothing springs to mind

My journal full of torment

My memories full of lies

I find my silver lining

In the glistening of a knife

I look out to a sunless sky

Obscured by the darkest clouds

A rain about to fall upon me

Thunder about to muffle my cries

And yet I can see the silver linings

That will temper my despair

Like the clouds, a world without me

Would be brightened once again

Hoping that someone would miss me

I look at faded photographs

A shadow of the man I was

A phantom of my past

I ponder on the right thing

The options that I weigh

As I slide the blade across my arms

And lay back and wait for hell

I look out to a sunless sky

Obscured by the darkest clouds

A rain about to fall upon me

Thunder about to muffle my cries

And yet I can see the silver linings

That will temper my despair

Like the clouds, a world without me

Would be brightened once again

I look upon the clouds

They look so different now

The silver on this side is total

With darkened linings around the edge

I feel free now of my feelings

My task is now complete

I lay back and wait for,

The ending, for my fate

I look out to a sunless sky

Obscured by the darkest clouds

A rain about to fall upon me

Thunder about to muffle my cries

And yet I can see the silver linings

That will temper my despair

Like the clouds, a world without me

Would be brightened once again

In hell I expected to wake

But my eyes are burnt with light

Heaven shouldn't hurt this much

I have found my own way back

The cries however are not mine

They are of those that truly cared

Those few people that I had forgotten

Who's stories I had made

I look out to a sunless sky

Obscured by the darkest clouds

A rain about to fall upon me

Thunder about to muffle my cries

And yet I can see the silver linings

That will temper my despair

Like the clouds, a world without me

Would be brightened once again

Still now I am not happy

My life just is not my own

The cries of the people around me

Are the linings that I looked for

A reason to continue

A mask to my disguise

Still now I am not happy

But I am a silver lining

In the shadow of the castle

Beside the castle walls even the largest of men look small

In the castles shadow broken men try to stand tall

Huddled together like cattle, trying to find some shelter

Shadows of their former selves they try to survive together

Lost and sickly gather those that are too poor

They live life free yet homeless beyond this large stone wall

In the shadow of the queen, homeless families huddle

Living out of damaged carts, packed together like cattle

Begging for scraps from passers by

Hoping for pennies for a meal

Those that have divert an eye

Careless of their ordeals

In the shadow of the queen, homeless women cry

As they watch their hopes and dreams die

In the eternal gaze of our oldest hero

These people are left to suffer

A man that once would have given to them

A trait he left to no other

He robbed from the rich and gave to the poor

Taking what those that had could afford

A legacy that has long since passed

Unlike the shadow of the castle walls.

Printed in Great Britain
by Amazon

20744670R00058